DISNEY·PIXAR

MONSTERS, INC.

Adapted by Andrea Posner-Sanchez

Illustrated by the Disney Storybook Artists

A GOLDEN BOOK • NEW YORK

randomhouse.com/kids
ISBN: 978-0-7364-2799-9
Printed in the United States of America
10 9 8 7 6 5 4

Monsters of all shapes and sizes lived in Monstropolis. The monsters kept their town running by sneaking into the human world and collecting screams from human children. Those screams were turned into energy.

Monstropolis was in the middle of an energy shortage. It was getting harder and harder to scare children.

Sulley and his best friend, Mike, worked at Monsters, Inc. Sulley was a Scarer. Mike was his assistant. Together they collected more screams than any other scare team.

Randall also worked at Monsters, Inc. He could blend into any background, making himself practically invisible.

Randall was the second-best Scarer at Monsters, Inc. He was always trying sneaky things to gather more screams than Sulley.

One day, Randall, Sulley, and the other Scarers stood in front of a row of doors, ready to start work. Each door would lead them into a different child's bedroom in the human world.

"May the best monster win," Sulley said to Randall.

"I plan to," Randall snarled back.

Randall worked fast and scared lots of children behind lots of doors. But when Sulley scared all the kids at a slumber party, he set a new scare record.

Everyone congratulated him—except Randall.

Uh-oh! A Scarer named George returned from a child's room with a sock stuck to his fur! Within seconds, special agents from the Child Detection Agency, known as the CDA, burst in and gave George a good cleaning. Monsters thought children—and their things—were toxic!

After the workday ended, Sulley noticed
that a child's door was still out on the Scare
Floor. He peeked inside but didn't see anyone.
As Sulley closed the door and started to walk
away, he heard a voice: "Kitty!"
A little girl was holding on to
his tail. She wasn't scared
of him—but he was
terrified of her!

Sulley panicked. He tried to get the girl back in her room, but she wanted to play. Sulley finally managed to hide her in a duffel bag just as Randall walked by. *Phew!* No one could know about the little girl. Human kids were not allowed in Monstropolis!

Sulley's secret didn't stay hidden for very long.

When he stopped in a restaurant to tell Mike what had happened, the little girl got out of the bag.

All the monsters in the restaurant screamed. Luckily, Mike and Sulley whisked the girl away before the CDA agents arrived.

    With no other place to go, Mike and Sulley took the little
girl back to their apartment. Mike put on all the protective
gear he could find. But Sulley was starting to think that
maybe the girl wasn't dangerous after all.

    And a very strange thing happened whenever she laughed:
all the lights glowed brighter than ever!

The next day, Mike and Sulley dressed the girl up like a little monster and went to work.

Everyone at Monsters, Inc.—even the boss, Mr. Waternoose—believed that the little girl was a monster child.

Mike and Sulley heard Randall and his assistant talking about the human girl. They realized that Randall was the one who had brought her to Monstropolis.

Mike and Sulley rushed to the Scare Floor. Mike tried to send the girl through the first door he saw, but Sulley stopped him.

"This isn't Boo's door," Sulley said.

Mike was shocked. Sulley had named the kid! Boo wandered away while the two friends argued.

As they searched for Boo, Mike and Sulley discovered that Randall had a plan to solve the energy shortage — he was going to use a machine to suck all the screams out of Boo! Sulley ran to tell Mr. Waternoose what Randall was up to. But Mr. Waternoose took Boo and pushed Mike and Sulley through a one-way door into the human world. Waternoose was in on Randall's wicked scheme!

The monsters ended up on a snowy mountaintop. Mike was furious with Sulley for getting them banished to the human world. But Sulley was worried about Boo. He quickly made a sled and sped down the mountain to a nearby village. Soon he found a kid's bedroom door and raced back into the monster world.

Sulley arrived at Monsters, Inc., just in time. Boo was already attached to Randall's machine. Sulley smashed the machine and ran off with Boo. Mr. Waternoose ordered Randall to get the girl back.

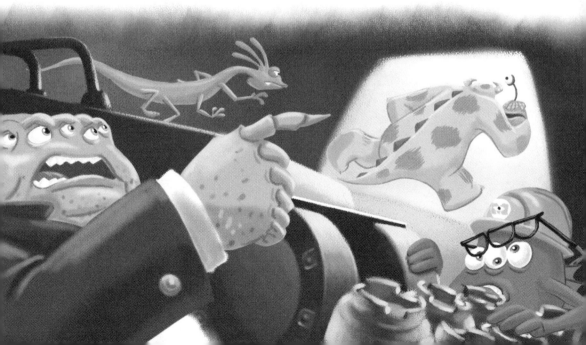

After a wild chase, Sulley, Mike, and Boo escaped from Randall. Then they tricked Mr. Waternoose into talking about his evil plan.

The CDA agents heard every word—and took Waternoose away. Boo was safe!

Mike had Boo's door waiting on the Scare Floor.

Sulley carried Boo into her room and tucked her into her
bed. "Nothing's coming to scare you anymore," he said to the
little girl. "Goodbye, Boo."

Sulley became the new boss at Monsters, Inc. Thanks to Boo, he had discovered that children's laughs created even more energy than their screams. Instead of scaring kids, the monsters showed up in their bedrooms and told them jokes. Mike quickly became one of the company's top Laugh Collectors.

The monsters were happy because their city had all the energy it needed. The children were happy because they weren't being scared at night anymore. And Sulley was happy because he could visit Boo whenever he liked!